Text copyright © 1990 by Mary Carmine.
Illustrations copyright © 1990 by Martin Baynton.

All rights reserved. Published by Scholastic Inc.,
730 Broadway, New York, NY 10003, by arrangement with
Ashton Scholastic Ltd.

SCHOLASTIC HARDCOVER is a registered trademark of Scholastic Inc.

Cataloging-in-Publication Data available.
Library of Congress number: 90-062708

ISBN 0-590-44638-X

12 11 10 9 8 7 6 5 4 3 2 1   1 2 3 4 5 6/9

Printed in Hong Kong
First Scholastic printing, February 1991

Daniel's Dinosaurs

BY
Mary Carmine

ILLUSTRATED BY
Martin Baynton

SCHOLASTIC
HARDCOVER

SCHOLASTIC INC.
New York

Ashley

Ashley B

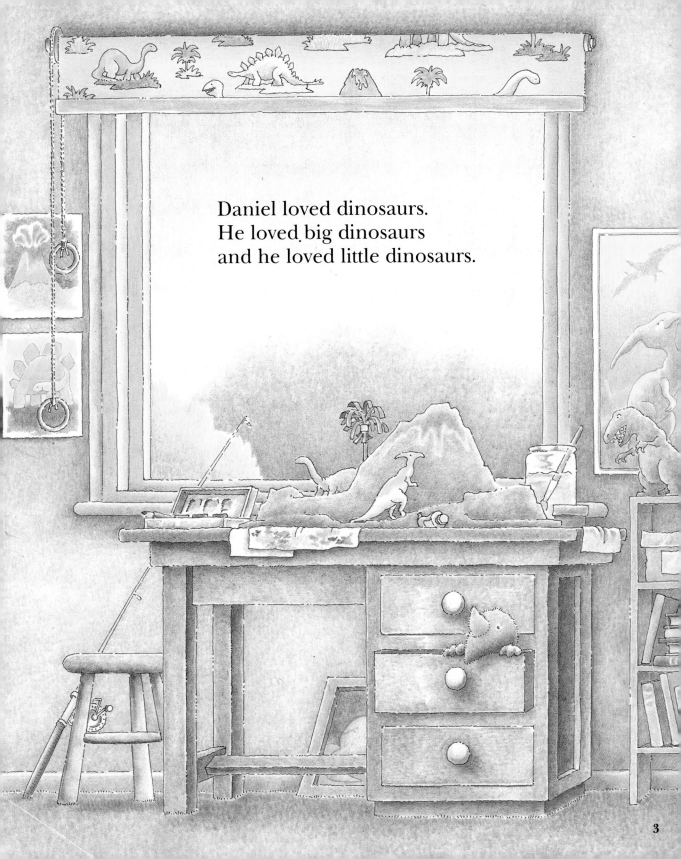

Daniel loved dinosaurs.
He loved big dinosaurs
and he loved little dinosaurs.

At the library,
he read books about dinosaurs.
When he drew pictures,
he drew pictures of dinosaurs.

When he wrote stories,
he wrote stories about dinosaurs.

Daniel's dinosaurs were everywhere.
Two Plateosaurs lived next door.

A Segnosaurus sat behind each check-out
at the supermarket.

An Allosaurus directed traffic,
and one unknown variety barked at him
from behind a high fence every morning
as Daniel passed by on his way to school.

Daniel's teacher
was a nice, friendly, plant-eating Diplodocus,
but sometimes . . .

13

she turned into
a big, fierce Tyrannosaurus!

"I wish you'd think of something else sometimes,"
said Daniel's mother.
"Why don't we go to the city
and visit the Aquarium?"

"That's a good idea," said Daniel.
"I like fish . . .
but not as much as dinosaurs."

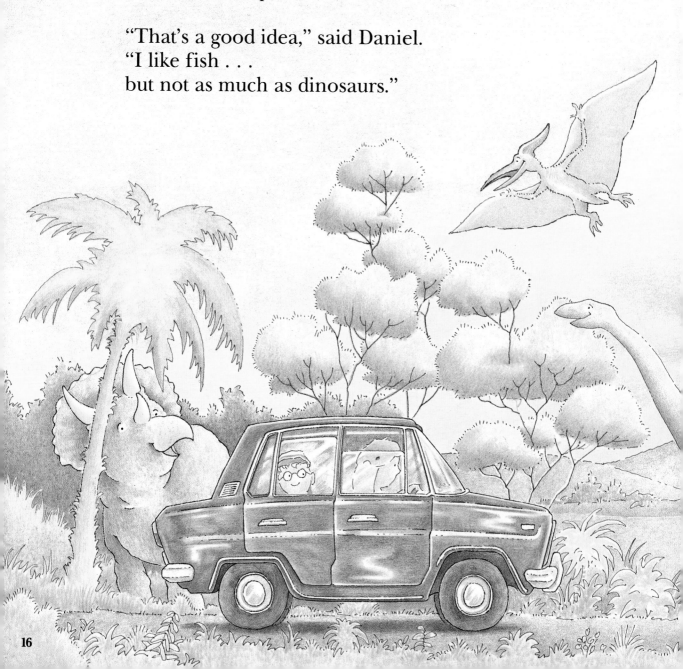

It was a long drive to the city.
All the way there,
Daniel drew pictures of dinosaurs.

A smiling Ceratosaurus took their money
at the ticket office.

Daniel and his mother looked at the rock pools,
the sea horses, and the little fish.

They looked at the stingrays . . .

and stayed for a long time.

They looked at the octopuses . . .

and stayed even longer.

Then they looked at the sharks . . .

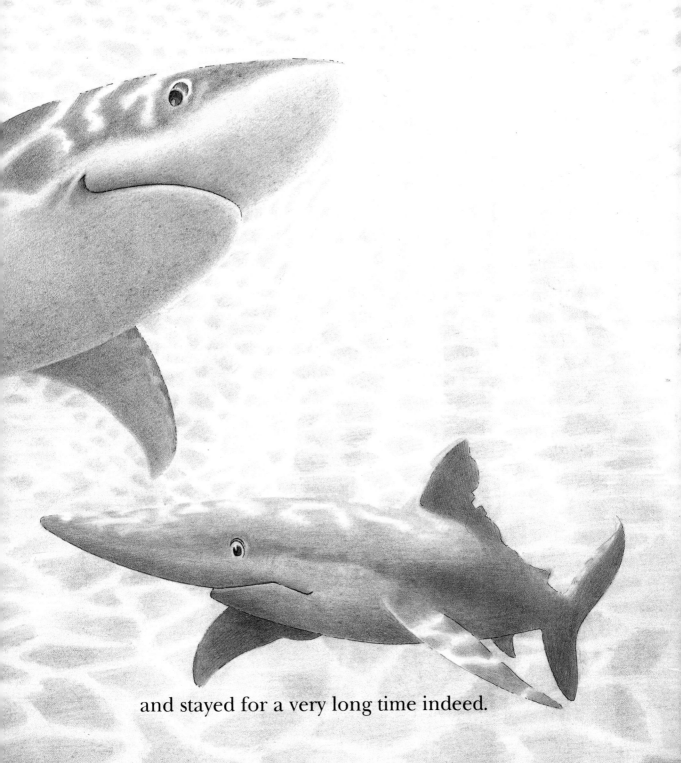

and stayed for a very long time indeed.

As they left, Daniel said goodbye
to the smiling, grey nurse shark
in the ticket office . . .

Glossary

Allosaurus (*al—o—saw—russ*)
A meat-eating biped (2-legged), heavily built and slow-moving, up to 12 metres long.

Ceratosaurus (*sir—at—o—saw—russ*)
The only meat-eating biped to have a horn on its nose, the Ceratosaurus was about 6 metres long.

Diplodocus (*dip—lod—a—kuss*)
A plant-eating quadruped (4-legged) and one of the longest known dinosaurs, measuring nearly 28 metres.

Plateosaurus (*plat—ee—o—saw—russ*)
A plant-eating dinosaur, up to 8 metres tall, which walked on either two or four legs.

Segnosaurus (*seg—no—saw—russ*)
A 4-metre long biped with webbed hind toes and a shortish tail, it is thought that the Segnosaurus may have lived by a river and fed on fish.

Tyrannosaurus (*tie—ran—o—saw—russ*)
The 'tyrant lizard', one of the fiercest dinosaurs, the Tyrannosaurus was a meat-eating biped, 14 metres long and 5 metres high, with more than 60 sharp teeth.